ush, Little Baby

A Folk Song with Pictures by Marla Frazee

BROWNDEER PRESS HARCOURT BRACE & COMPANY   San Diego   New York   London

ACKNOWLEDGMENT

This book was researched at Fort New Salem, West Virginia,
where living history programs interpret the Appalachian heritage of 1790 to 1901.
Special thanks to Nora Edinger of Salem-Teikyo University,
Carol Schweiker, the director of Fort New Salem, and to the rest of the gang—
Sharon the artisan, Sean the cook, Dawn, Becky, and "Chuck" (who had just turned 13)—
for their West Virginian hospitality.

Browndeer Press is a registered trademark of Harcourt Brace & Company.

Library of Congress Cataloging-in-Publication Data
Hush, little baby: a folk song with pictures/by Marla Frazee.
p. cm.
"Browndeer Press."
Summary: In an old lullaby a baby is promised an assortment of presents from its adoring parent.
ISBN 0-15-201429-2
1. Folk songs, English—Texts. [1. Lullabies. 2. Folk songs.]
I. Frazee, Marla, ill.
PZ8.3.H9535 1999
782.42162'21'00268—dc21
[E]   98-9608

First edition
A C E F D B
Printed in Singapore

The illustrations in this book were done in acrylic artist's ink and
black Prismacolor pencil on Strathmore two-ply kid finish paper.
The type was set in Celestia Antique.
Color separations by United Graphic Pte. Ltd., Singapore
Printed and bound by Tien Wah Press, Singapore
This book was printed on totally chlorine-free Nymolla Matte Art paper.
Production supervision by Stanley Redfern and Ginger Boyer
Designed by Kaelin Chappell and Marla Frazee

To Tim, my yoke-mate,
for three of the sweetest little reasons in town

Hush, little baby,

don't say a word,

Papa's gonna buy you

a mockingbird.

If that mockingbird

don't sing,

Papa's gonna buy you

a diamond ring.

If that diamond ring

is brass,

Papa's gonna buy you

a looking glass.

If that looking glass

gets broke,

Papa's gonna buy you

a billy goat.

If that billy goat

don't pull,

Papa's gonna buy you

a cart and bull.

If that cart and bull

turn over,

Papa's gonna buy you

a dog named Rover.

If that dog named Rover

don't bark,

Papa's gonna buy you

a horse and cart.

If that horse and cart

fall down,

You'll still be the sweetest

little baby in town.